TIM AND
CHARLOTTE

by
Edward Ardizzone

For my niece, Charlotte

Scholastic Children's Books
Commonwealth House, 1-19 New Oxford Street,
London WC1A 1NU, UK
a division of Scholastic Ltd
London ~ New York ~ Toronto ~ Sydney ~ Auckland
Mexico City ~ New Delhi ~ Hong Kong

First published by Oxford University Press, 1951
First published in hardback by Scholastic Ltd, 2000
This paperback edition published by Scholastic Ltd, 2002

Copyright © Edward Ardizzone, 1951

ISBN 0 439 01038 1

Printed and bound in Belgium

2 4 6 8 10 9 7 5 3 1

The right of Edward Ardizzone to be identified as the author and
illustrator of this work has been asserted by the Estate of Edward Ardizzone
in accordance with the Copyright, Designs and Patents Act, 1988.

One day Tim and Ginger were walking along the beach near Tim's house.

The weather was stormy and Tim and Ginger were happy because they liked to

watch the great waves crashing on the beach and feel the strong wind and salt sea spray on their faces. They liked, too, to run

races with the big waves as they rushed into the shore.

On their way they stopped to talk with Tim's friend the old boatman.

"Dirty weather," he said, "and it will get worse. I pity them poor lads at sea."

"Ooh," said Tim with a shiver, "something exciting is going to happen. I feel it in my bones."

The old boatman was right. As they went on, the wind blew harder and the waves became bigger. Suddenly Tim gave a great

shout. "Ginger, what's that in the water? Oh, it is a little girl, quickly, we must rescue her."

They dashed into the sea and pulled her out.
She lay very still and quiet on the beach.

She had on a lifebelt. Her eyes were closed and she was breathing gently as if she was asleep.

Between them they carried her to their house close by.

Tim's mother put her to bed with lots of hot water bottles and blankets.

She then sent for the doctor and told Tim
and Ginger to change their wet clothes.

The doctor gave the little girl a thorough
examination. "Hm!" he said. "The girl is

in a faint. Keep her warm and quiet. She
should soon come to."

For a long time the girl lay with her eyes
shut, not moving at all.

Tim and Ginger took it in turns to watch by the bedside, so that somebody would be there when she woke up.

Ginger became rather tired of watching and said he thought that girls were a bore.

At last she opened her eyes. Tim was there at the time.

"Oh!" she said, "Where am I?" "You are all right," said Tim and went to call his mother and Ginger.

Then they asked her lots of questions such as – What is your name and where do you come from? But to all this she only answered, "I'm so sorry, I don't know."

Tim's mother told the girl to lie still and not to bother, then she said to the boys, "I hear father coming in, let's have a family conference. I fear the poor child has lost her memory."

At the conference they decided to call the girl Charlotte because Tim liked the name. Ginger thought of some silly names like Fishy and Seaweed, but I am afraid he was rather jealous.

Then they wrote a
notice which was
later printed

FOUND WASHED
UP BY SEA
GIRL ABOUT
5 YEARS OLD
SUFFERING FROM
LOSS OF MEMORY
CURLY HAIR
BLUE EYES
WEARING
PINK FROCK
LIFE BELT

APPLY A
SEA VI

and pasted up on walls and fences about
the town.

However, the weeks went by and nobody
answered the notices.

Soon Charlotte was well enough to get up. She proved to be a dear little girl. She was kind, helpful and willing, and had very good manners.

She loved to work in the house and Tim's mother taught her how to sew, darn, peel potatoes, bake cakes, make beds and lots of other useful things.

Tim found her a very
good playmate and it was
only Ginger who was not
quite happy.

What a
fuss about
a silly
girl

He had the sulks
and refused to play
with them.

One day, when they least expected it, a large car drew up at the gate of Tim's house. An elderly lady got out of the car and entered the garden.

Tim and Ginger were watching. They felt sure that something exciting was going to happen and they were right. For no sooner had Charlotte seen the lady than she gave a great cry – "Aunt Agatha! Oh, now I remember who I am."

Soon they were all in the drawing room
listening to Charlotte's story.

She told them that curiously enough her
real name was Charlotte and that she was
very rich, but had no father and mother and
lived instead with her guardian, whom she
called Aunt Agatha.

She told them, too, how one day she was on the deck of her Aunt's yacht when she fell overboard.

The Aunt then described how they had looked and looked for Charlotte in the stormy sea but could not find her and how in the end they had given her up for lost.

You see, they did not know that she was wearing her lifebelt.

When all the story had been told, Aunt Agatha got up and said, "Now Charlotte, go and get ready to come home with me."

Charlotte begged to be allowed to stay because she was fond of Tim and liked helping with the housework.

But Aunt Agatha said no she must
remember she was a rich girl and must
return to the big house where she belonged.

Tim was sad, too, when he waved
goodbye.

Charlotte's house was very large and very grand.

When she and Aunt Agatha arrived, the cook, the butler and the other servants were in the hall to greet her.

She was pleased to see the cook whom she liked very much.

As soon as Charlotte had taken off her hat and coat she ran upstairs to her big nursery.

There she found all her old toys. There
were lots and lots of them.

Now you would think that with lots of

money, a big house and all her toys
Charlotte would have been happy but I'm
afraid she wasn't. She was very sad.

The trouble was that she was lonely and missed Tim and Ginger and the fine games they used to play.

Aunt Agatha was kind, but not nice and kind in the way Tim's mother was.

As the days went by Charlotte became

sadder and sadder. Often she would sit for hours on her rocking horse, rocking backwards and forwards, thinking of Tim and his house by the sea.

Aunt Agatha was quite cross when she used to see her pale sad face.

"Now Charlotte, don't mope"

Sometimes Charlotte would slip down to
the kitchen and help her friend the cook
make pastry. She was happiest then. But
Aunt Agatha did not like it and, when

she found her there, would say, "Really, Charlotte, the kitchen is no place for you. You must learn to be a lady. Off to your room, Miss."

Poor Charlotte! Not only did she become more sad, but pale and thin too.

Aunt Agatha was worried and called the doctor.

"The child wants a tonic," said the doctor,

Say Aah

but the days went by and the tonic did no good.

Then Aunt Agatha called a more expensive doctor who said, "Give her pills three times a day." But the pills did no good and Charlotte became so pale and thin that she had to go to bed.

At last Aunt Agatha called a third doctor who was even more expensive than the second one.

This doctor was very kind. He sat by
Charlotte's bed and asked her all sorts of
questions about herself.

She told him about Tim and Ginger and their house by the sea and how she longed to go back there.

When the doctor left her she heard him talking to Aunt Agatha in the next room.

She heard Aunt Agatha sniff and say something about wild boys and an unsuitable family.

Charlotte wondered what it was all about.

Now you must not imagine that poor Charlotte was the only person who was sad. Tim was sad because he missed her and so were Tim's mother and father and even Ginger, in spite of the fact that he was still a little jealous.

They all loved her and wished she was with them.

But Tim had another reason for being sad. He was teased at school.

Some of the boys had found him writing a letter to Charlotte and had taken it from him. They read it out loud and after that kept saying horrid things about him and her.

One day Tim became so angry that he

said he would fight the lot of them, and
that was how a very famous battle started,

which was talked about for years to come.
The battle was known as 'Tim's Last Stand'.

Ginger rushed to help Tim and between them they did noble deeds that day.

Tim knocked down big Mick, the strongest boy in the school. He hit Smithers the bully so hard on the nose that he ran away crying "Oh! Oh! Oh!"

He threw down Charlie and Dick and Peter, all jolly good fighters.

Ginger wrestled very well and though he was knocked down several times he got up to fight again.

In the end there were too many boys against them. They became tired and were nearly beaten.

"I am done for, Ginger," gasped Tim; but at that very moment the school bell rang for lessons and they were saved.

As you can imagine, Tim and Ginger were in a terrible state. Tim had a black eye and Ginger was bruised and scratched and both had torn clothes.

After school they crept towards home,

but when they got near they had a surprise
which made them forget all about their
bruises and scratches.

Waiting for them at the garden gate
was Charlotte.

Soon they
were all in the
kitchen. Charlotte
bathed Tim's eye, Tim's mother looked
after Ginger and they all talked and talked
and talked.

Tim told them about the fight. Charlotte
felt rather proud that it was about her.

Charlotte told them how she had been ill

and how the kind doctor had said that she must come and stay with them for always, though her aunt did not like it a bit, but had to agree.

"Phew," said Tim, as he and Ginger went to bed that night, "I am tired, what an exciting day it has been."

Curiously enough, after the battle, the boys at school no longer teased Tim. They became quite friendly with both him and Ginger.

When Tim told them about Charlotte

they all said that it was a very good thing.

Ginger, too, gave up being silly and grew to like Charlotte more and more.

Their happiest times, however, were when they played together on the beach, bathing, climbing about the boats, talking to the old boatman, or telling each other stories. Both Tim and Ginger had been to sea before and Charlotte was never tired of listening to the tales of their adventures.

— *The End* —